Special Thanks to Kathy Holte, Chandra Lydeen, and Elizabeth Marroquin, without whom this book would not be possible!

Edited by Lily Coyle

ISBN 13: 978-1-59298-684-2
Library of Congress Catalog Number: 2015916191
Printed in the United States of America
First Printing: 2016
20 19 18 17 16   5 4 3 2 1

Beaver's Pond Press, Inc.
7108 Ohms Lane
Edina, MN 55439–2129
(952) 829-8818
www.BeaversPondPress.com

To order, visit www.ItascaBooks.com
or call (800) 901-3480. Reseller discounts available.

www.melissamarroquinillustration.com

Tide Day

Written and Illustrated by
Melissa Marroquin

"It's a Tide Day! Wake up!" said Pearl's mother.

"But a Tide Day means no school," Pearl grumbled.

"The rip tide has shifted too close to the school, but you still have jellyfish chores to do!"

"Chores are the **worstest**," said Pearl.

"Worstest is not a word," replied her mother.

"Is **dullest** a word?" asked Pearl.

"How about **crummiest**?"

"Is biggest-pains-in-my-fins-iest a word!"

"Naughtiest is a word!" said Pearl's mother. "Now you are on time-out until you are ready to apologize to the jellyfish for saying such mean things about them."

All Pearl could think about was how she'd rather spend her day playing with her speediest, funniest, and shiniest friends.

So that's what she did.

"Hello! Do you want to come out and play with me?"
Pearl asked the speedy seahorses.

"Play in the rip tide?" gasped the first seahorse.
"And get sucked out into the deep?" said the next.
"We'll stay in the seaweed and play tag instead!"
said the third.

"But I'm too big to play in the weeds. The weeds are
the worstest," said Pearl.

"The worst, you mean," said all the seahorses.

"I'll go see the crabs," said Pearl.
"They're the funniest!"

"Sorry, Pearl," said a crab. "The rip tide is not funny at all! Stay here and build rock forts with us!"

"Rocks are the worstest," sighed Pearl.
"Worstest isn't a word," said a crab.

"You will come play with me, won't you?" she asked the shiny octopus.
"And tangle my tentacles in the rip tide? Absolutely not!" he said.

Pearl still wanted to go out and play.

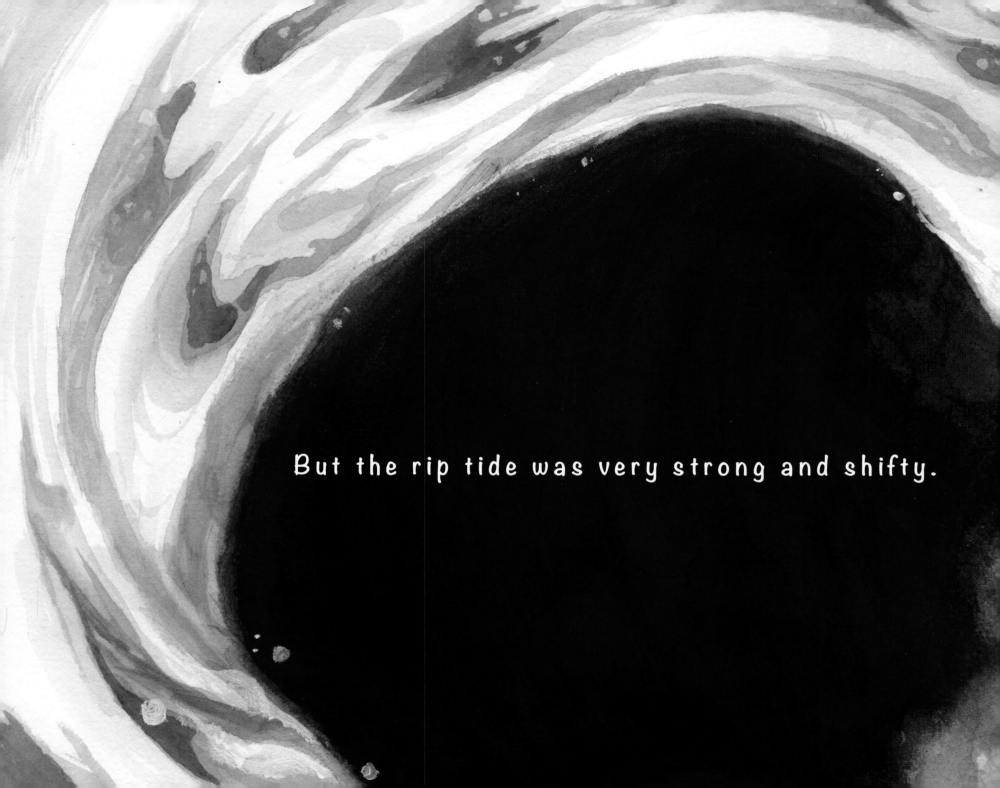

But the rip tide was very strong and shifty.

"Okay," said Pearl, "I think I am done now."

"I'm getting dizzy..."

"Let me go, please!"

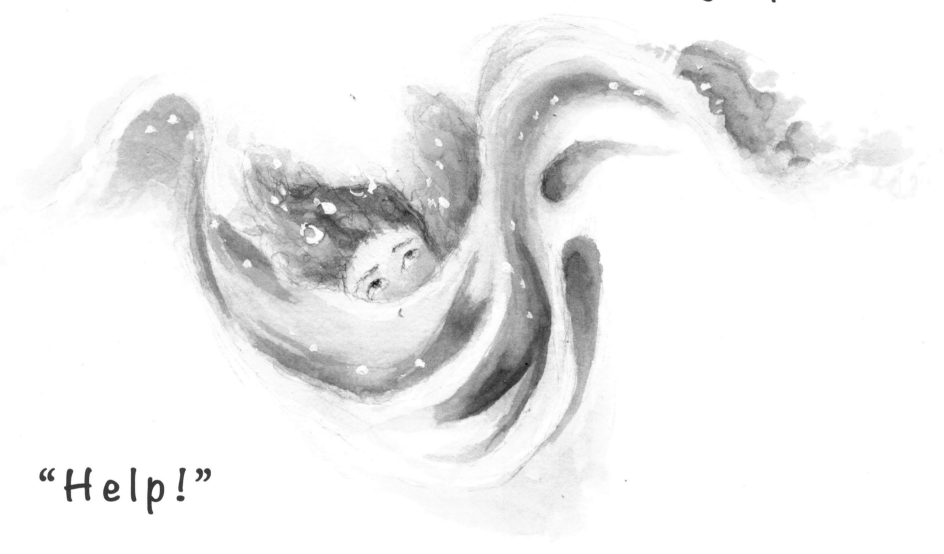

"Help!"

Poor Pearl was caught.

The jellyfish heard Pearl,

and twirling, twisting, and whirling, they came!

The jellyfish carried Pearl backed to the calm deep.

"Mom, jellyfish are
the bestest!"

"Bestest is not a word," said her mother.

"Okay, how about **best?**"

Melissa Marroquin began her career as an illustrator at the age of six with a marker in hand and the vast canvas that was the back of the living room sofa.

A large family and the adventures they encountered gave Melissa a love for story telling that, combined with her developing skills, drew her to the Minneapolis College of Art and Design, as well as the College of Visual Arts in Saint Paul.

There, she acquired a BFA in Illustration and specializes in Children's Books. Now, Melissa lives in Roseville with her Co-adventurer and with her delightful cat Luna.